HI-TECH JOBS WITHOUT COLLEGE

BE A SOCIAL MEDIA COORDINATOR

by Samantha S. Bell

BrightPoint Press

San Diego, CA

BrightPoint Press

an imprint of ReferencePoint Press, Inc.
Printed in the United States

For more information, contact:
BrightPoint Press
PO Box 27779
San Diego, CA 92198
www.BrightPointPress.com

LIBRARY OF CONGRESS CATALOGING-IN-PUBLICATION DATA

Name: Bell, Samantha S., author.
Title: Be a social media coordinator / by Samantha S. Bell.
Description: San Diego, CA: ReferencePoint Press, Inc., 2025 | Series: Hi-Tech Jobs Without College | Audience: Grade 7 to 9 | Includes bibliographical references and index.
Identifiers: ISBN: 9781678209407 (hardcover) | ISBN: 9781678209414 (eBook)
The complete Library of Congress record is available at www.loc.gov.

CONTENTS

AT A GLANCE

- Social media allows people to form online communities.
- There are many social media platforms. Each one has different features.
- A social media coordinator manages the social media accounts of a business or brand.
- Social media coordinators must be skilled in writing, creativity, and organization.
- Special software helps social media coordinators keep up with the demands of their jobs.
- Social media coordinators spend time each workday creating content and engaging with their audience.

- There are many ways to learn how to be a social media coordinator. These include online classes, internships, and more.

- Social media coordinators must keep up with changing trends.

POSTING WITH A PURPOSE

Lanae Spruce walked down the sidewalk in Washington, DC. Spruce, who uses they/them pronouns, made their way through the Monday-morning crowd. They were on their way to the National Museum of African American History and Culture. Spruce works there as a social media coordinator. Their job is to promote the museum on social media.

Social media coordinators help shape an organization's public image.

When they arrived at their office, Spruce got to work. They began by reading the news. They had to stay up to date on things. They also had to know about the latest trends. Their job is to make posts about these things. They write from the museum's point of view.

Spruce looked at their computer. There were no big news stories that day. But the Fourth of July was coming up. Spruce decided to share some history about the holiday.

The US national anthem is called "The Star-Spangled Banner." It's about an American flag that flew over Fort McHenry in 1814. Spruce had heard an interesting story about the flag. They knew that a white woman sewed the flag. Teenage

The National Museum of African American History and Culture opened in 2016.

girls helped her sew it. Spruce learned that one of the girls was Black. Her name was Grace Wisher. Wisher was usually left out of the story.

Spruce made a post about Wisher. Posts like this start conversations among the museum's followers. Spruce's posts are a way for the museum to share history.

In January 2023, 79 percent of internet users in the United States used social media at least once.

Their words also remind followers to visit the museum.

WHAT IS A SOCIAL MEDIA COORDINATOR?

Social media coordinators like Spruce use social media to promote **brands** and organizations. They do this by posting on social media platforms. They talk to their followers in comments.

Everything that coordinators post is with their brand in mind. Posts draw attention to the brand and build an audience. Posts may also raise sales. The goals of the brand are reflected in the **content** that coordinators make. Successful coordinators represent their brand well.

EXPLORING SOCIAL MEDIA

Social media allows people to share ideas online. People do this by making posts on social media platforms. A social media platform is an online service on which users can interact.

There are many different social media platforms. Examples include Facebook, X (formerly Twitter), and TikTok. Others are YouTube, Snapchat, and Instagram.

Smartphones provide many people with access to social media.

Social
TikTok
Instagram
Facebook
3
LinkedIn
Business Suite
18
YouTube

These are all online spaces where people can share things.

People share all kinds of things on social media. They make written posts. They upload photos and videos. Some people share details about their personal lives.

Smartphone cameras allow people to take pictures and post them to social media using the same device.

For example, they might write about their travels or hobbies. They might post photos of their family. Some people post their opinions. They write about trends or current events. Organizations also use social media. Their posts are more professional. They may post about events, products, or other information related to their mission.

FEATURES AND RULES

Each social media platform has different features. For example, Facebook is for text, photos, and videos. X is for short text posts, photos, and videos. Instagram is a photo- and video-sharing site. TikTok users post videos. Different platforms are used in different ways. Many people keep up with family and friends on Facebook.

Users follow news stories as they develop on X. Instagram allows users to create an online visual identity. The most popular use for TikTok is entertainment.

Sometimes the features of a site change with new technology. For example, Facebook began as a site for sharing text and photos. Today, it allows people to **live stream** events as they are happening. X started with a limit of 140 characters, or written symbols, per post. The limit was set because of the technology available. But it became the most well-known feature of the platform. Eventually, the technology improved. The posts increased to 280 characters. People who subscribe to X Premium can write even longer posts.

Each platform also has its own set of rules. People who want to share their ideas must follow the platform's rules. Those who don't will not be allowed to use the platform. They will no longer be a part of that online community.

WHO USES SOCIAL MEDIA?

Different platforms appeal to different users. Facebook began as a site for

Age Limits

People must be 13 years old to sign up for most social media sites. This is because of the risks of using social media. People may be bullied online. They may see inappropriate content. They could be influenced to make bad decisions. It is important to use social media wisely.

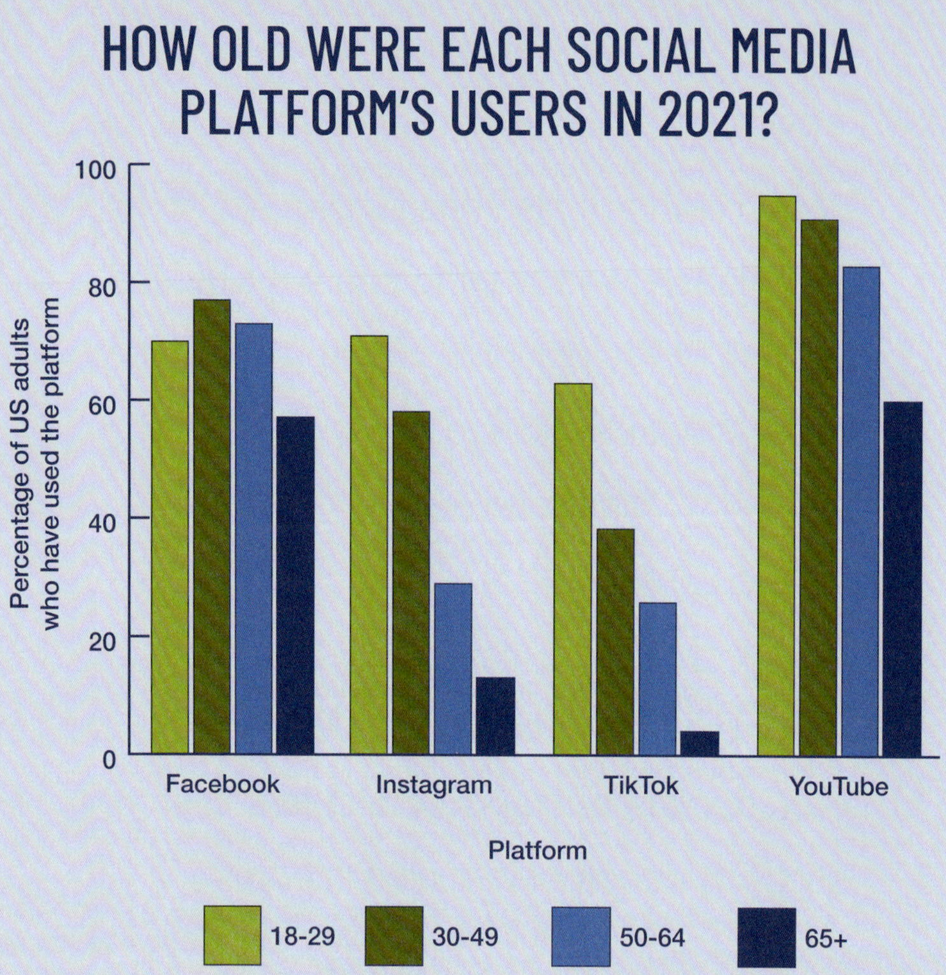

Source: Brooke Auxier and Monica Anderson, "Social Media Use in 2021," Pew Research Center, *April 7, 2021. www.pewresearch.org.*

The graph above shows the percentage of US adults in different age groups who said in 2021 that they ever use certain social media platforms.

college students. It was a place where they could talk to each other. Now adults of all ages use Facebook. People who use X are more likely to be young adults. Many of them have gone to college and live in cities. Instagram appeals to teens and young adults. Most TikTok users are between the ages of 18 and 24.

Organizations use many different social media platforms. They use social media as a marketing tool. It is a good way to bring people to their websites. They use it to promote products. Social media also helps them create their brand. They use it to let people know what they stand for.

WHAT DOES A SOCIAL MEDIA COORDINATOR DO?

In 2023, about 4.8 billion people worldwide were using social media. More than $200 billion was spent to advertise on it.

Abdul Muhammad worked at a marketing agency in Florida. He explained, “People are on social media all day, every day. Brands must go where the people are.”[1] Companies want to stand out to all these people. To do so, they often hire a social media coordinator. This position is also called social media manager or specialist. The social media coordinator runs the social media accounts of a company. They represent the company online. They talk to the public for the company.

Social media coordinators make posts the same way regular users do. They may post text, images, or videos. The content is made to get people interested in the company. Coordinators also follow other conversations on the platforms.

In 2022, about 268 million Americans spent money online.

Sometimes social media coordinators from different companies collaborate over the internet.

They respond to posts. They talk with their customers. Amy Jo Martin owns a company that helps other businesses with social media. She said, "It's a dialogue, not a **monologue**, and some people don't understand that. Social media is more like a telephone than a television."[2]

Sometimes coordinators work with people from other companies. They may **collaborate**. This could involve supporting each other's ideas and causes. They might work on a team together. Or they may simply comment on one another's posts.

Using social media is about having conversations. It is about being part of a community. Social media coordinators help companies start these conversations. They help companies build communities with customers and clients. It's a social media coordinator's job to make these online connections.

CHAPTER TWO

TRAINING FOR THE JOB

Social media coordinators benefit from having certain skills. They must know how to use social media platforms. They must be creative content producers. And they need to know the interests of their audience. There are many ways to learn these skills. Social media coordinators can even learn some skills on their own.

Coordinators first must know how to use different social media platforms.

Social media coordinators need basic computer skills in order to succeed.

They should understand how each one works. They can do so by making a personal account on each platform. That way, they can get hands-on experience.

It is important to think carefully before posting on a platform. Other people will

Social media coordinators must be good copywriters. In marketing, the term *copy* refers to the text that appears in advertisements.

see the post. This can include future employers. When a person applies for a job, employers will often search for their social media accounts. The employers want to know more about the person. They want to be sure the person fits in with the company. Sometimes, people post things that could turn employers away. They may post something offensive. They may complain about their job. They might argue with others online. Employers are looking for people who are professional. They want to see what they can do with social media.

OTHER SKILLS

One important task for social media coordinators is creating written content. This means that coordinators should be good writers. Written content includes captions, posts, and blogs.

When writing, coordinators must keep in mind their brand. Their writing represents the brand. It should communicate the brand's values. This doesn't mean that the writing has to be formal. Many brands use humor on social media. Coordinators study how people talk online. Then they use fun tones in their writing. This makes brands more relatable to people.

Writers must also think about who they want to read the text. These readers are called the target audience. The writer tries to connect with the target audience. They create content especially for those readers. They must know what their readers expect.

Popular video editing software includes Adobe Premiere Pro and Final Cut Pro.

And they need to know what their audience wants.

Visual content is also important. Visual content includes images and videos. Gifs and memes are popular examples of visual content. Coordinators must be creative. They must design visual posts that catch people's attention. They hope people will share them with others.

Online courses may include previously recorded or live lectures.

Coordinators must think of exciting ways to present content. This is especially true if they have shared similar content before. Lanae Spruce said, “We’ve told the story a million times before. But we're always looking for a new angle, a new way to keep people **engaged**."[3]

WHERE TO LEARN

Many types of organizations use social media. This means that there are many different ways to become a social media coordinator. There is not one single path to take.

One way to learn about social media is to take online courses. Some courses are free. Others cost hundreds of dollars. These courses cover many different topics. For example, some courses teach people how to use social media platforms. Others teach people how to reach a certain target audience.

People may earn certificates from courses. A certificate shows that they have a certain skill. To earn a certificate, people may have to take exams. When they pass the exams, they earn the certificate.

The company HubSpot offers a free social media course. People can take it at a pace they choose. It teaches basic social media marketing skills. These include how

More Ways to Learn

In 2009, Michael Stelzner did not know much about social media marketing. But he was a quick learner. That year, he created a website called Social Media Examiner. He invited people to share things about social media marketing. Today, the site also features a YouTube channel and hosts several podcasts.

Preparing for job interviews is a necessary part of earning any professional position.

to create a social media strategy. They also include how to grow an audience. People earn a certificate at the end of the course.

Another way to gain experience is to attend a boot camp. A boot camp is a short, in-depth training program. People in boot camps become skilled at using social media in only a few months. The training prepares them to apply for jobs later.

People usually need work experience to become social media coordinators.

Some people gain experience through internships. An internship is a temporary job. Internships can help people hone their social media skills.

People get hands-on experience during an internship. Sometimes interns get paid for their work. Others do it only for the

For some social media coordinators, all they needed to get the job was a high school diploma.

work experience. This experience will help when they begin looking for a job.

Some people gain experience by volunteering. They may work for a nonprofit organization. Or they may help someone with a personal project. Other people start out with an entry-level job. These are jobs for people who do not have much experience.

Some people earn college degrees to become coordinators. They may earn degrees in marketing or communications. But a college degree is not required for coordinators. A person can learn how to manage social media in many other ways. Employers are looking for people who have proven their skills. They want people who can connect with an audience online.

CHAPTER THREE

WORKING IN THE FIELD

Social media coordinators work online. They can work anywhere with an internet connection. Some companies want coordinators to work in the office. Other companies let them work from different places, such as their home. This is known as working remotely.

The most important tool for coordinators is a computer. This may be a desktop or

Some remote workers enjoy working from cafés.

laptop computer. Many coordinators also create content on smartphones.

To stay organized, coordinators use special software. Some of these programs help them keep track of their accounts. These programs are known as social media management tools. They have many useful features. Coordinators can use them to schedule posts for later. The tools can show all the company's accounts in one place. They also show how many people engaged with the posts.

Coordinators may also use a content calendar. They use these calendars to plan what content they will post. The calendar helps them decide when to post it.

Social media coordinators use **analytics** tools, too. These tools help them see how

Analytics tools typically present information in tables and graphs.

well their posts do. They give information about how many comments a post received. They also show how many people were reached. Coordinators use these reports to make better content. They can also use them to prove how well their strategies work.

Popular photo editing software includes Photoshop and Lightroom.

SOFTWARE FOR CREATING

Coordinators use many other programs. Some of these programs help them make posts. For example, they may need to include a link to a website. But sometimes website addresses are long. Coordinators can use programs to shorten them. This is helpful when posting on X. Shorter links work better with the character limits.

Other types of programs help create images. Canva is a popular program of this kind. Many people use it to design eye-catching posts. The program includes many photos, graphics, and tools.

Coordinators also work with videos. Programs help them edit the videos. They can add special effects. They can add music or other audio. They can also change the speed of the video. Rearranging video clips is also possible.

A TYPICAL WORKDAY

Many people use social media to relax. But not social media coordinators. Mitra Mehvar is a social media manager. She works for a social networking company. She said, "Being a social media manager can mean a seriously busy day of work. Although from the outside it may look like we're just having fun scrolling through TikTok all day, we're actually doing lots of different tasks!"[4]

Many coordinators can choose their work schedules. They know what they need to do during the day. They decide when they will do each task. For example, Mehvar begins

Producing videos for social media may require a set. This is a constructed space where videos are filmed.

by reading emails. Other coordinators start differently. Rita Ovis worked as a social media coordinator for a company that sells air-freshening products. The first thing she did each day was post on her company's Facebook and Instagram pages.

Every morning, Mehvar spends time engaging with her company's audience. She checks the comments on posts. Then she replies to each of the comments.

Hashtags

Users can use hashtags to link their content to a topic, event, or theme. Hashtags help people find the content they want. Social media coordinators often collect the best hashtags for their brand. Then they have the hashtags ready when they need them.

She also checks for direct messages. These are private messages between two social media users. Direct messages are another way social media users can talk to organizations. Sometimes users reach out to companies on social media with questions. For example, a customer may need help using a company's product. Coordinators might need to help such customers.

Mehvar also checks to see if her company was tagged in a post. Tagging is a feature of some social media platforms. It is a way to mention other users in a post.

The rest of the day can be just as busy. Coordinators have many other tasks to do. Ovis explained, "I usually spend my day rounding up and creating content to share

Many workers benefit from using calendars to schedule their time.

on all of our platforms, interacting with our followers and **influencers**, and working on any other projects I have going on."[5]

Mehvar has found she works best if she focuses on one task at a time. There is always something happening online. It is easy to become distracted. To avoid this, Mehvar sets aside time for certain tasks. She sets aside time for learning. She also makes sure she has time for creating.

LOOKING AHEAD

Social media coordinators will likely have many job opportunities in the future. More people are using social media. Companies want to reach them. This means that companies will use social media more as well. The demand for coordinators will continue to increase. The average salary for a social media specialist is around $52,000 a year. Managers of a company's

In 2023, the average person spent about 2.5 hours a day on social media.

social media strategy earn around $70,000 a year.

CHANGING PLATFORMS

Technology is always changing. Coordinators must keep up with the changes. Some people may find this difficult. Others think of it as fun. Rachel Strella works in social media management. She said, "Rather than cringe at what

Live video is a popular social media technology.

technology has in store for us, we need to keep cool heads. The one constant we can always count on is change."[6]

New technology can change social media platforms. The technology gives people new ways to post. For example, Facebook Live Audio launched in 2021. It allows users to broadcast audio live. People can join to listen. Teens and young adults especially enjoy the audio content. It gives them a new way to express themselves.

Sometimes platforms choose not to use the technology. Facebook's audio launch also included podcasts. Users could listen to podcasts on Facebook. Podcast creators could add parts of episodes on their timelines. But 10 months later, Facebook ended support for podcasts. The company decided to go in a different direction. Social media coordinators had to make changes too.

Platforms can change for other reasons. Sometimes social media platforms are sold. The new owner might make changes to the platform. For example, in 2022, Elon Musk bought Twitter. He changed its name to X. Some of the policies changed as well.

Taking Off with Short-Form Videos

Short-form video is a popular type of video content. It is usually filmed vertically. The videos are usually between 5 seconds and 3 minutes long. Short-form videos can be shared on many social media platforms. Social media coordinators are using them to make their organizations stand out.

Elon Musk bought Twitter for $44 billion.

For example, people or businesses could pay to go over the character limit.

Companies want to use social media platforms that are safe for their brand. Sometimes companies choose to stop using a certain platform. In 2023, comments by Musk on X caused **controversy**. Many businesses decided to leave X. Coordinators must be ready to respond to controversy. They still represent their company. They have to figure out what is best for their brand.

New social media platforms are also being created. People are trying out these new platforms. Social media coordinators are too. Threads is a text-based social media app. It was created to compete with X. People talk about things by writing short messages. People can also link their Threads and Instagram accounts. Threads was launched in July 2023. Within 10 days, it had 100 million active users.

CHANGING TRENDS

Social media coordinators must keep up with social media trends. A trend is a topic that spreads quickly among people. Trends appear, draw a lot of interest, and then fade.

To keep up with social media trends, coordinators have to pay close attention to what is popular online at any given moment.

Many people review products and services on social media.

Coordinators can use trends to engage their audience.

Coordinators also have to watch how people use social media. For example, many people search for information using social media instead of search engines. They are looking for products, reviews, and recommendations. This is especially true among teens and young adults. Prabhakar Raghavan is a leader at the company Google. He said, "In our studies, something like almost [40 percent] of young people, when they're looking for a place for lunch, they don't go to Google Maps or Search. They go to TikTok or Instagram."[7]

People shop on social media, too. Instagram was one of the first social media platforms to add shopping. Some experts believe other platforms will do the same. Coordinators will have to change their strategies. For example, one report showed that teens and young adults like to find new products in videos. Coordinators will need to make videos to reach this audience.

Many social media users also want to be authentic in their posts. They want to be who they truly are online. This has led to the popularity of apps such as BeReal, which encourages its users to present authentic versions of themselves. Users want companies to be authentic, too. Briana Rabiola is a social media manager for a nursing association. She said, "I think audiences want a peek behind the curtain. They want to take a look at the people and processes behind a brand."[8]

People who enjoy using social media to draw people's attention should consider a career as a social media coordinator.

Social media coordinators are experts at their jobs. But changing trends show there is always more to learn. Coordinators must stay on top of what is happening. They must always look for ways to connect with their audience.

GLOSSARY

analytics

information that comes from examining data

brands

public identities of people, products, services, or companies

collaborate

to work with someone else on a project

content

information posted on social media with the intent to entertain or engage

controversy

a public matter of disagreement

engaged

interacting with something

influencers

people with considerable followings on social media who advertise products

live stream

to transmit live video or audio over the internet

monologue

a long speech given by a single speaker

SOURCE NOTES

CHAPTER ONE: EXPLORING SOCIAL MEDIA

1. Quoted in David Cotriss, "Social Media for Business: Marketing, Customer Service and More," *Business News Daily*, January 17, 2024. www.businessnewsdaily.com.

2. Quoted in Steve Kearns, "7 Quotes to Inspire Social Media Marketing Greatness in 2022," *LinkedIn Ads Blog* (blog), *LinkedIn*, January 12, 2022. www.linkedin.com.

CHAPTER TWO: TRAINING FOR THE JOB

3. Quoted in Elka Torpey, "Social Media Specialist," *Career Outlook* (blog), *US Bureau of Labor Statistics*, November 2016. www.bls.gov.

CHAPTER THREE: WORKING IN THE FIELD

4. Mitra Mehvar, "A Day in the Life of a Social Media Manager: How to Spend Time on Social Media in 2024," *Buffer*, March 27, 2023. www.buffer.com.

5. Quoted in Louise Miller, "Meet the Team: Rita Ovis, Social Media Coordinator," *Natural Habitat* (blog), *Vitruvi*, n.d. www.vitruvi.com.

CHAPTER FOUR: LOOKING AHEAD

6. Rachel Strella, "4 Tips to Help You Keep Up with the Constant Changes in Social Media," *Social Media Today*, January 16, 2019. www.socialmediatoday.com.

7. Quoted in Erica Santiago, "The Future of Social Media [Research]: What Marketers Need to Know," *Marketing* (blog), *HubSpot*, May 29, 2023. https://blog.hubspot.com.

8. Quoted in "10 Social Media Marketing Trends for 2024 [+ Experts Share Their Thoughts]," *Influencer Marketing Hub*, November 14, 2023. www.influencermarketinghub.com.

FOR FURTHER RESEARCH

BOOKS

Holly Bathie, *Social Media Survival Guide*. London, England: Usborne, 2022.

Dionna L. Mann, *The Genius of Facebook: How Mark Zuckerberg and Social Media Changed the World*. Minneapolis, MN: Lerner, 2023.

Roxanne Troup, *Jobs If You Like Social Media*. San Diego, CA: BrightPoint Press, 2025.

INTERNET SOURCES

"9 Skills You Need to Become a Great Social Media Manager," *Digital Marketing Institute*, August 30, 2023. www.digitalmarketinginstitute.com.

"Social Media Coordinator, University of Maryland Eastern Shore," *Candid Career*, n.d. www.candidcareer.com.

"When Is Your Brain Ready for Social Media?," *PBS*, July 20, 2019. www.pbs.org.

WEBSITES

GCF Global
www.gcfglobal.org

GCF Global offers free online courses in many topics, including social media.

HubSpot Academy
https://academy.hubspot.com

HubSpot Academy provides free courses in social media marketing and other subjects.

Social Media Magazine
www.socialmediamagazine.org

Social Media Magazine helps social media managers engage with customers, market products, and grow their brand.

INDEX

IMAGE CREDITS

ABOUT THE AUTHOR

Samantha S. Bell lives in the foothills of the Blue Ridge Mountains with her family and lots of cats. She has written more than 150 books for students in elementary through high school. She has also created numerous social media posts for businesses. It's quite a job!